Topsy + Tim

go to the park

Jean and Gareth Adamson

Blackie

Copyright © 1991 Jean and Gareth Adamson
First published in 1991 by Blackie and Son Limited

British Library Cataloguing in Publication Data
Adamson, Jean, 1928—
Topsy and Tim go to the park
I. Title   II. Adamson, Gareth, 1925–1982
823'.914 [J]

ISBN 0-216-93139-8
ISBN 0-216-93138-X Pbk

Blackie and Son Limited
7 Leicester Place
London WC2H 7BP

Printed in Hong Kong by
Wing King Tong Co. Ltd.

One sunny day, Topsy and Tim
and Mummy set off for the park
with a picnic for themselves and
two big bags of bread for the ducks.

The ducks were pleased to see
Topsy and Tim.

Feeding the ducks had made
Topsy and Tim feel hungry.
'Let's go and find a place to
have our picnic,' said Mummy.

They ate their picnic sitting
on a park bench. Topsy had
peanut butter sandwiches, crisps
and some orange juice.
Tim had marmite sandwiches,
crisps and apple juice.

When they had finished, there
was a lot of rubbish left.
'What do we do with that?'
said Mummy.
'Put it in the bin!' shouted
Topsy and Tim.
'Let's go to the swings now,'
said Tim.
'I'll race you there,' said Topsy,
and off they ran.

When they reached the playground,
it was already full of children.
All the swings were taken.

'Hello, Topsy and Tim,' called
someone high in the air. It was
their schoolfriend Kerry on one
of the swings.
'Hello, Kerry!' called Topsy,
running towards her.

Kerry's mum grabbed Topsy
and pulled her back.
'You nearly got bumped on
the head,' she said.
'You must never go close to
swings,' said Mummy.

It wasn't long before Topsy
and Tim and Kerry were having
lovely swings together, all in
a row.

'Now let's have a go on the seesaw,' said Tim, when they were tired of swinging. Topsy and Kerry sat at one end of the seesaw and Tim sat at the other, but Tim got stuck up in the air.

The seesaw wouldn't work with
all three on it together, so they
had to take turns. Then they all
went down the slide together.

At last they had had enough
fun in the playground. They
wandered back to the grassy
part of the park.
'I wish we'd brought a ball
to play with,' said Tim.

'Surprise, surprise,' said Kerry's
mum and she opened her bag and
tipped out a big, bouncy ball.
Soon Tim and Kerry and Topsy
were hot and happy, playing
ball on the grass.

Suddenly a big dog came running across the grass. It caught the ball in its mouth and leaped around with it.

'Drop it!' said Tim in a stern
voice. The dog dropped the ball
and stood wagging its tail.
'Good dog,' said Tim and he put
out his hand to pat the dog.
'Don't touch the dog, Tim,' said
Mummy. 'You must never pat a
strange dog. It might bite you.'

'I wish that dog would go away,'
grumbled Topsy. 'It's spoiled
our game of football.'
Just then the dog heard its
owner calling. It gave a cheerful
bark and ran off.

'It's time to go,' said Mummy.
Topsy and Tim waved goodbye to
Kerry and her mum and they all
began to walk back to the park gates.

On the way, they had to pass
the park cafe.
'I'm very hot,' said Tim.
'I'm boiling,' said Topsy.
'Would an ice cream cool you
down?' asked Mummy.
'Ooh, yes,' said Topsy and Tim.

Topsy and Tim and Mummy ate their
ice creams as they walked through
the park. When they went past the
pond, a crowd of ducks waddled
after them, hoping for a bit of
cornet.

'Sorry, ducks, it's all gone,'
said Topsy.
'But we'll bring you lots more
bread next time we come,'
promised Tim.